Little Owl's Orange Scarf

by

Tatyana Feeney

OXFORD
UNIVERSITY PRESS

Little Owl lived with his
Mummy in a tree house
on the edge of the City Park.

He loved
doing sums,

eating ice-cream,

and riding his scooter.

He usually loved
surprises, but . . .

he did not love his new scarf.

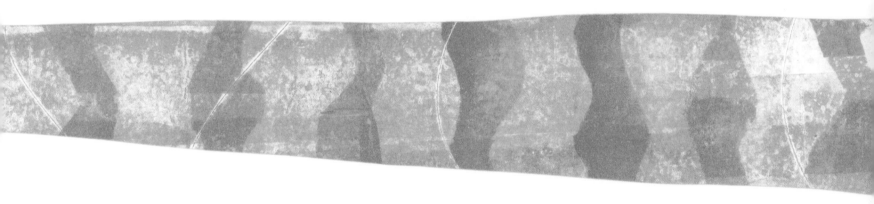

It was itchy.

It was too long.

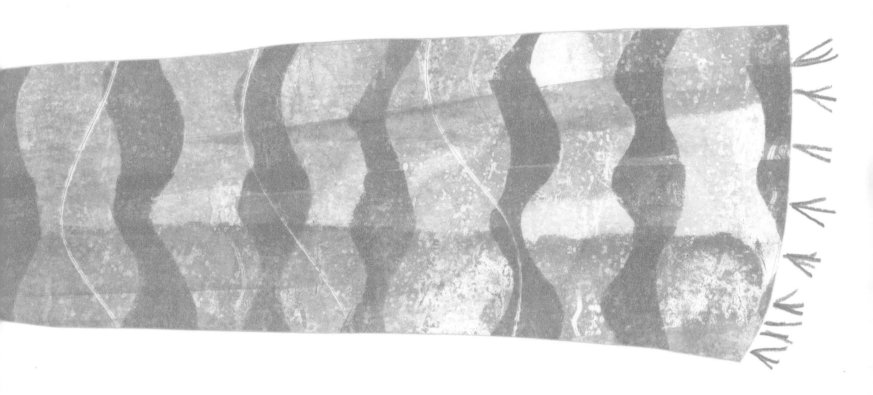

It was far too orange.

'You need to wear your new scarf,' said Mummy. 'It will keep you nice and warm.'

Little Owl tried very hard
to lose his new scarf.

But Mummy always found it.

'You'll need to wear your scarf today,' said Mummy. 'It's your class visit to the zoo.'

Little Owl came home from
the zoo with all sorts of stories.

But Little Owl came home from the zoo **without** his scarf.

Mummy rang the zoo.
Nobody had found Little Owl's scarf.

'Never mind,' she said,
'we can make another scarf . . .

and this time we will
do it together!'

The wool shop was more
exciting than Little Owl expected.

After a lot of hard work,
Little Owl's scarf was finished.

It was soft.

It was just long enough.

It wasn't orange.

Little Owl loved it . . .

. . . especially on visits to the zoo!

To Niall

OXFORD
UNIVERSITY PRESS

Great Clarendon Street, Oxford OX2 6DP

Oxford University Press is a department of the University of Oxford.
It furthers the University's objective of excellence in research, scholarship,
and education by publishing worldwide in

Oxford   New York

Auckland   Cape Town   Dar es Salaam   Hong Kong   Karachi
Kuala Lumpur   Madrid   Melbourne   Mexico City   Nairobi
New Delhi   Shanghai   Taipei   Toronto

With offices in

Argentina   Austria   Brazil   Chile   Czech Republic   France   Greece
Guatemala   Hungary   Italy   Japan   Poland   Portugal   Singapore
South Korea   Switzerland   Thailand   Turkey   Ukraine   Vietnam

Oxford is a registered trade mark of Oxford University Press
in the UK and in certain other countries

Text and illustrations © Tatyana Feeney 2013

The moral rights of the author/illustrator have been asserted

Database right Oxford University Press (maker)

First published in 2013

British Library Cataloguing in Publication Data available

ISBN: 978-0-19-279454-3 (hardback)
ISBN: 978-0-19-279455-0 (paperback)

2 4 6 8 10 9 7 5 3 1

Printed in China

Paper used in the production of this book is a natural,
recyclable product made from wood grown in sustainable forests.
The manufacturing process conforms to the environmental
regulations of the country of origin